BROWN RABBIT'S
BUSY DAY

LITTLE RABBITS

ALAN BAKER

KINGFISHER

NEW YORK

KINGFISHER
LONDON & NEW YORK

First published by Kingfisher 1994
This edition published 2017 by Kingfisher
Published in the United States by Kingfisher,
175 Fifth Ave., New York, NY 10010
Kingfisher is an imprint of Macmillan Children's Books, London.
All rights reserved.

Copyright © Alan Baker 1994

Distributed in the U.S. and Canada by Macmillan,
175 Fifth Ave., New York, NY 10010

Library of Congress Cataloging-in-Publication data
has been applied for.

ISBN: 978-0-7534-7337-5 (HB)
ISBN: 978-0-7534-7356-6 (PB)

Kingfisher books are available for special promotions
and premiums. For details contact: Special Markets
Department, Macmillan, 175 Fifth Ave.,
New York, NY 10010.

For more information, please visit
www.kingfisherbooks.com

Printed in China
9 8 7 6 5 4 3 2 1
1TR/1216/WKT/UG/157MA

Early one morning,
Brown Rabbit found
his favorite recipe book
beside his bed.
It gave him a good idea.

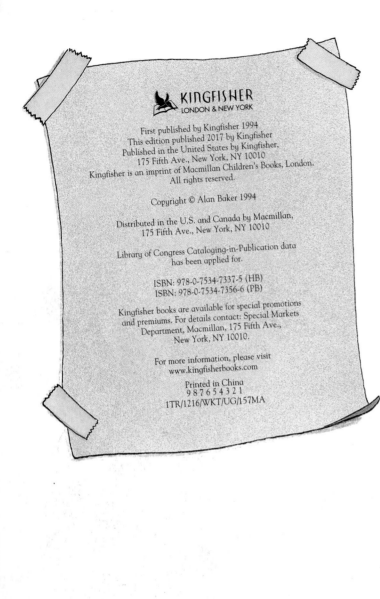

SALADS IN SECONDS

HEALTHY HERBIVORE

RECIPES FOR BUSY BUNNIES

THE 5-DAY SPINACH DIET

THE SLIMMER RABBIT COOKBOOK

JUST JELLIES!

ETABLE COOKING FOR ONE

RECIPES
ROVENCE

BEANS FOR BEGINNERS

UTES

ANING
REENS

At breakfast time
he wrote notes
to his friends.

To
White
Rabbit

After breakfast
he found some
Jell-O molds.

Then slowly and carefully he made four batches.
First, a plum purple Jell-O.
Second, a dandelion yellow Jell-O.
Third, a lettuce green Jell-O.
Last, a radish red Jell-O.

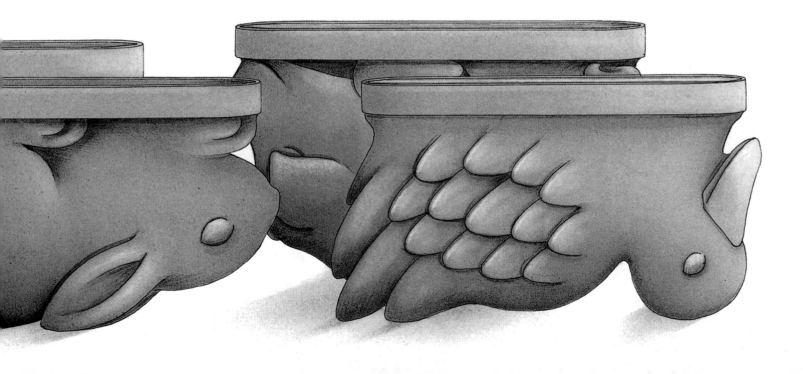

Brown Rabbit left the Jell-O to set and went
to fetch strawberries, radishes, dandelion
flowers, and other good things to eat.

He kept testing the Jell-O
to see if it was ready.
Hurry up, Jell-O!
he thought.

At lunchtime Brown Rabbit
ate a big juicy apple.

Then he tested the molds again. At last they were set. Brown Rabbit carefully turned them out. A plum purple pig. A dandelion yellow duck. A lettuce green hen and a radish red rabbit.

They looked delicious!

Brown Rabbit
decorated them
with fruit
and vegetables.

He was just finishing
the final decorations
when . . .

...his friends
arrived
to play.

First they played hopping.
Watch out, Brown Rabbit!

Then they played leaping.

Be careful with your paws, Brown Rabbit!
All afternoon they played until...

... it was time to eat the Jell-O.
Jell-O with dandelion flowers,

Jell-O with strawberries, Jell-O with radishes, and Jell-O with lettuce. Delicious!

Thank you, Brown Rabbit,
said his friends sleepily
as they waved
good-bye.

How fast time goes when
you're having fun,
he thought.

What a busy day.
Goodnight, Brown Rabbit!